*To you, because one day you will become
that wonderful father you dream of being.*

Alicia Acosta

*To Javier.
To my mother who taught me
that boys too could play with dolls.*

Luis Amavisca

To my adorable sweethearts: Rachid, Jonas and Léna.

Amélie Graux

ÉGALITÈ

Benji's Doll
Egalité Series

© Text: Alicia Acosta and Luis Amavisca, 2021
© Illustrations: Amélie Graux, 2021
© Edition: NubeOcho, 2021
© Translation: Robin Sinclair, 2021
www.nubeocho.com · hello@nubeocho.com

Original Title: *La muñeca de Lucas*
Text Editing: Caroline Dookie, Rebecca Packard

First Edition: October 2021
ISBN: 978-84-18133-40-4
Legal Deposit: M-31702-2020

Printed in Portugal.

Benji's Doll

Alicia Acosta & Luis Amavisca

Illustrated by
Amélie Graux

Benji wanted a doll. He wanted one really badly.

He asked for one for Christmas and for his birthday. He even broke his piggybank to throw his coins in the "Fountain of Wishes"!

Jenny, his best friend, had a really pretty doll,
with beautiful long blue braids.

They loved playing together. Jenny shared her doll with Benji, and in exchange, he lent her his truck.

They had so much fun!

One day, Mom and Dad gave Benji
a big box wrapped in a shiny ribbon.

He opened it, and...

His wish had come true!

Inside the box was a beautiful doll,
with big green eyes and red hair.

Benji couldn't wait to show
his new doll to Jenny!

While they were sitting in the park, their friend Eva came by.

"Benji, are you playing mommies and daddies?" she asked.

"Yes, do you want to play with us?"

But then Pablo came along and snatched the doll from Benji.

"Give it back!" Benji screamed.

Pablo wouldn't listen. He squeezed the doll's head until it started swelling like a balloon, as if it was about to...

Benji hugged his doll and cried.

"Don't worry, we will love her the same," Jenny and Eva said.

Pablo felt very bad. He just wanted to play, he didn't mean to break the doll.

A couple days went by, and they saw Pablo again. He carried a ball under his arm and something in his hand.

"Hi..." Pablo said.

Benji didn't answer and he hid his doll.

"Benji, I am really sorry about the other day,
and I brought you something."

"Are you going to make fun of me?" Benji shouted.

"No, I'm not, I promise. Please, take it."

When Benji opened the box,
he found a nice surprise.

"An eyepatch for my doll! Thanks, Pablo!"

That afternoon, Jenny, Eva, Pablo and Benji
played football and hide-and-seek in the park.

And of course,
they also played with their dolls...

THEIR PIRATE

DOLLS!!!